MY COLOR IS PANDA

MY COLOR IS PANDA

Deborah Winograd

GREEN TIGER PRESS

PUBLISHED BY SIMON & SCHUSTER
NEW YORK LONDON TORONTO SYDNEY TOKYO SINGAPORE

GREEN TIGER PRESS
Simon & Schuster Building
Rockefeller Center
1230 Avenue of the Americas
New York, New York 10020
Copyright © 1993 by Deborah Winograd
GREEN TIGER PRESS is an imprint of Simon & Schuster.
Designed by Sylvia Frezzolini.
Manufactured in the United States of America.

10 9 8 7 6 5 4 3 2 1

Library of Congress Cataloging-in-Publication Data
Winograd, Deborah.   My color is panda / by Deborah Winograd.
p.   cm.
Summary: A panda pretends to be the colors of
the different plants in his habitat.
1. Colors — Juvenile literature. [1. Color.   2. Pandas.]
QC495.5.W57   1993   92-17423
535.6 — dc20   CIP
ISBN: 0-671-79152-4

For Pete's sake

My name is Panda

**and this is
my friend Mr. Skunk.**

I wonder how it would feel
to be ORANGE like a poppy

or **PURPLE** like grapes

or GREEN like bamboo

or YELLOW like daffodils

or **RED** like a rose?

How would it feel
to be moonglow BLUE?

I have **BLACK** and WHITE fur.
What color am I?

My color is PANDA!